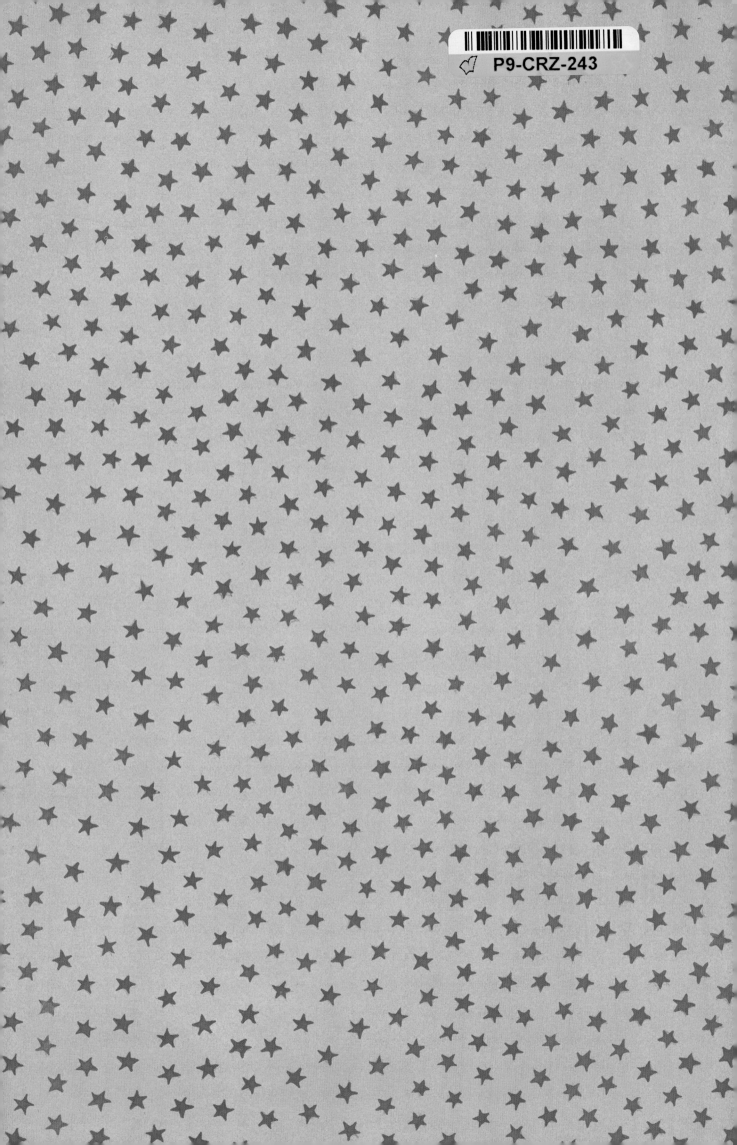

SANTA CLAUS
The
WORLD'S NUMBER ONE TOY EXPERT

Marla Frazee

Harcourt, Inc.

Orlando   Austin   New York   San Diego   Toronto   London   North Pole

For Allyn, one of the elves

Requests for permission to make copies of any part of the work should be mailed
to the following address: Permissions Department, Harcourt, Inc.,
6277 Sea Harbor Drive, Orlando, Florida 32887-6777.

www.HarcourtBooks.com

Library of Congress Cataloging-in-Publication Data
Frazee, Marla.
Santa Claus: the world's number one toy expert/Marla Frazee.
p.   cm.
Summary: Santa Claus has his own ways of knowing more about
children and toys than anyone else in the world.
[1. Santa Claus—Fiction.   2. Gifts—Fiction.   3. Christmas—Fiction.]   I. Title.
PZ7.F866San   2005
[E]—dc22   2004005228
ISBN 0-15-204970-3

C E G H F D B

Printed in Singapore

The illustrations in this book were done in black pencil and gouache
on Strathmore paper, hot press finish.
The display and text lettering were created by Marla Frazee.
Color separations by Bright Arts Ltd., Hong Kong
Printed and bound by Tien Wah Press, Singapore
This book was printed on totally chlorine-free Stora Enso Matte paper.
Production supervision by Ginger Boyer

No one knows more about kids
than Santa Claus.
He is the world's
number one
kid
expert.

He meets a lot of kids.
He listens to them.
He visits with the brave ones who hop
right up on his lap.

He watches the shy ones who don't.

And he even has his own Santa Claus ways of getting to know kids who never have a chance to meet him in person.

He takes lots and lots of notes,

compiles all his research,

and works
long, long hours
the whole year round.

Nothing makes him happier.

No one knows
more about toys
than Santa Claus.

He is the world's number one toy expert.

He finds the best toys in the whole world.

He makes sure they are fun to play with.

He checks them out to see if they are sturdy.

Or not.

He even has his own Santa Claus ways of making the cozy toys become **EXTRA** special.

He carefully inspects each toy,

makes the final selections,

and works
long, long hours
the whole year
round.

He loves his job.

No one knows more about gifts than Santa Claus.

He is the world's number one gift expert.

When it is almost Christmas, Santa thinks very hard about all the kids he knows so well.

He thinks very hard about all the toys he's played with.

He works carefully
to match up
each particular toy
with each
particular
kid.

He changes
his mind
many times, and...

after hours and hours of very hard work, he gets it all figured out.

And then
on Christmas morning,
Santa Claus gives the
exact right toy
to the
exact right
kid,

99.9 % of the time.

That's almost always!

(Well, no one is perfect. Not even Santa Claus.)

Then when the day is over
and all his work is finished,
Santa Claus goes home and unwraps
the special gift
he picked out
for
himself.

And it's almost always just exactly what he wanted.

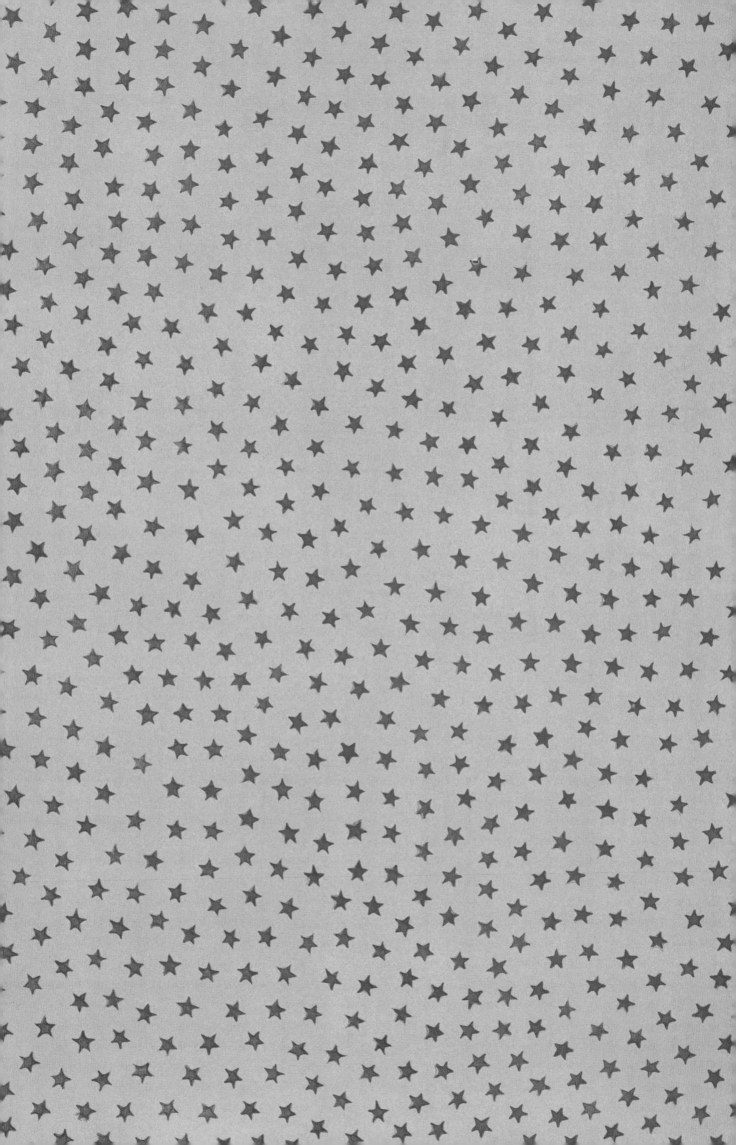

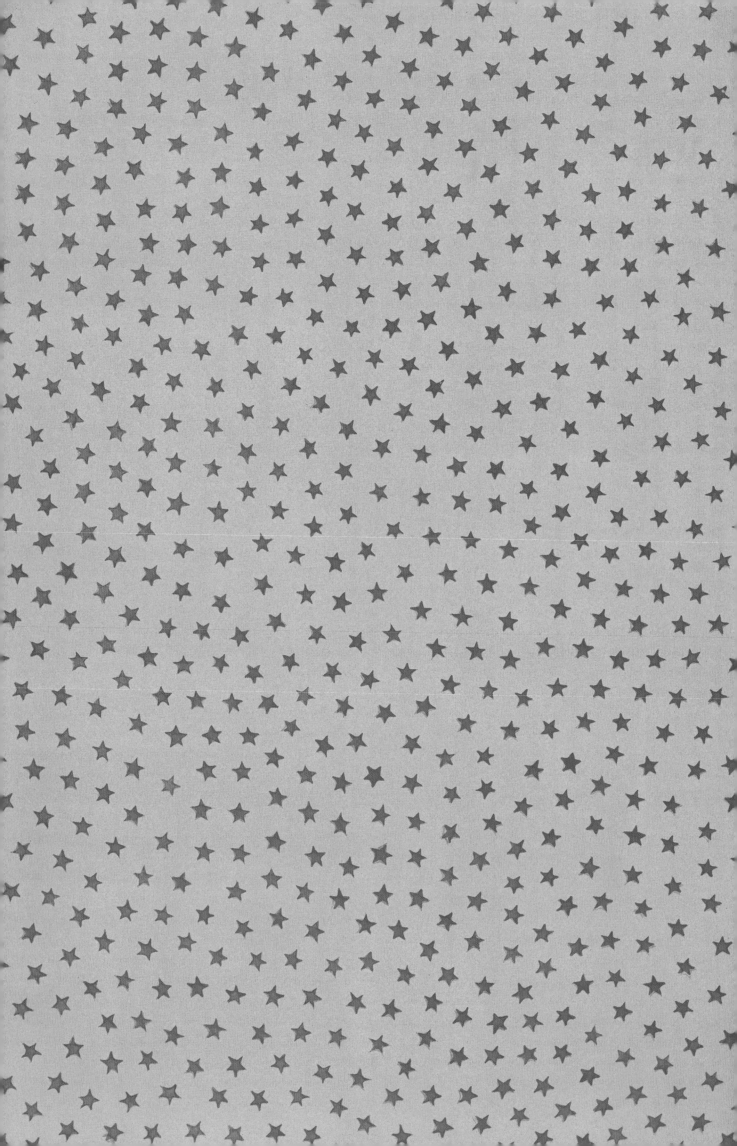